Zoe the Magic Love Dog

By Carrie Hauman

ALMA PRESS

LOS ANGELES

For Otto

Special Thanks to Gerard Bourgeois, Howard Craig, Judy Dye,
Constance Hauman, Bailey Humes, and Alana.

Published by Alma Press
520 Washington Blvd. #630
Marina del Rey, CA 90292
www.almapress.com

The text is set in Tophat
The paintings in this book are oil on canvas

Printed in Korea
First Printing 2003

Library of Congress Control Number 2003097544
Hauman, Carrie
Zoe the Magic Love Dog/written and illustrated by Carrie Hauman
Alma Press
Summary: Zoe spreads love and healing to children throughout the world.

ZOE THE MAGIC LOVE DOG

paintings and verse by Carrie Hauman

In an orange house near a field full of flowers...

lived a dog named Zoe, whose tail had magic powers.

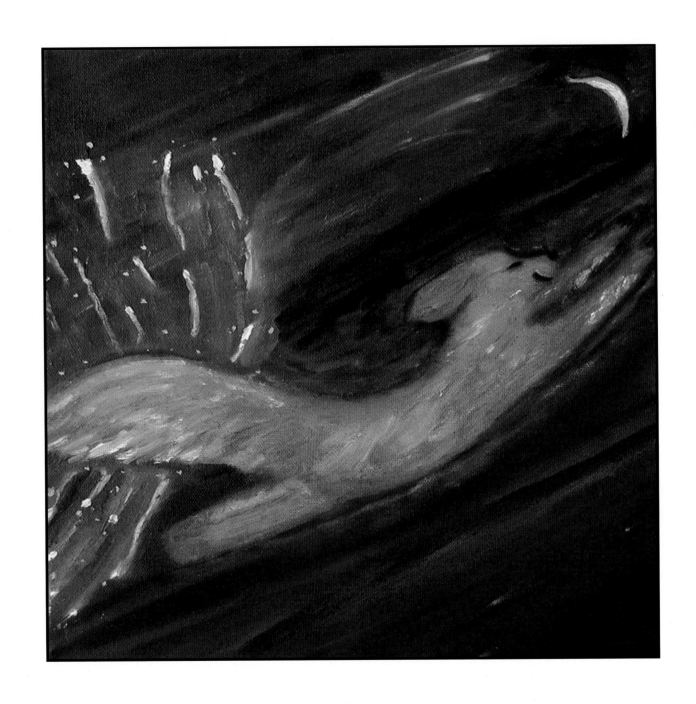

And with those powers she could fly...

and flip and twirl...

through the sky.

She loved to dance.

She loved to surf.

She loved to shop with a hat and purse.

Her cat, Meemo, was always there...

to make sure Zoe had good care.

Playing "Go Fish" was lots of fun...

and so was napping in the sun.

But one night, when Zoe took flight...

she knew something in the world was not right.

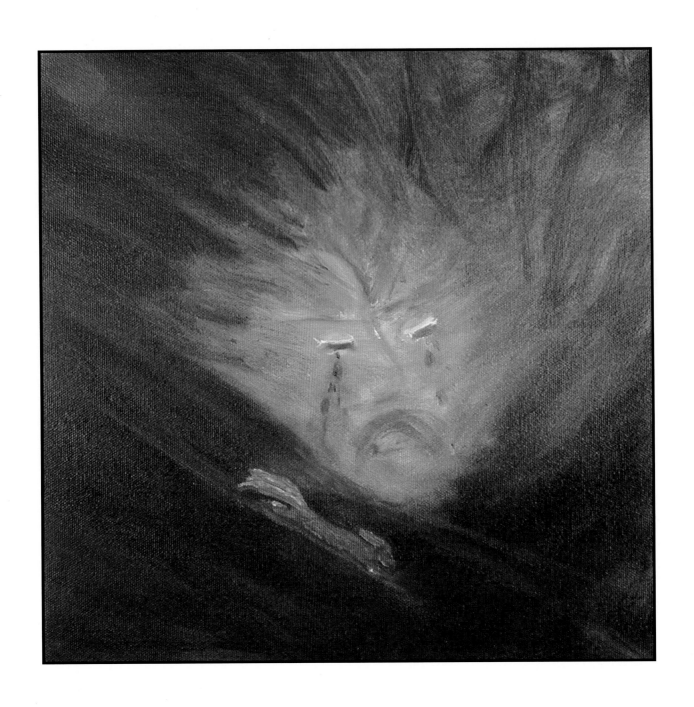

A deep sadness filled the air...

that was almost too much for Zoe to bear.

And so she took on a special mission...

to heal the world with love's nutrition.

The first place she would start was in each and every child's heart.

She often healed them in their dreams...

but certain kids required other schemes.

A little girl who would not share
was in desperate need of Zoe's care.

And after only several hours...

she felt the healing of Zoe's powers.

Next, Zoe found a little boy who never seemed to have any joy.

His life was sad. He missed his dad.
His mom worked late. He rarely ate.

So Zoe taught him how to laugh.

She even helped him with his math.

And late that night in the clear moonlight,
the little boy knew everything would be all right.

Zoe smiled at a job well done. Giving love is really fun.

She sends you lots of love and light.

And wishes you a sweet goodnight.